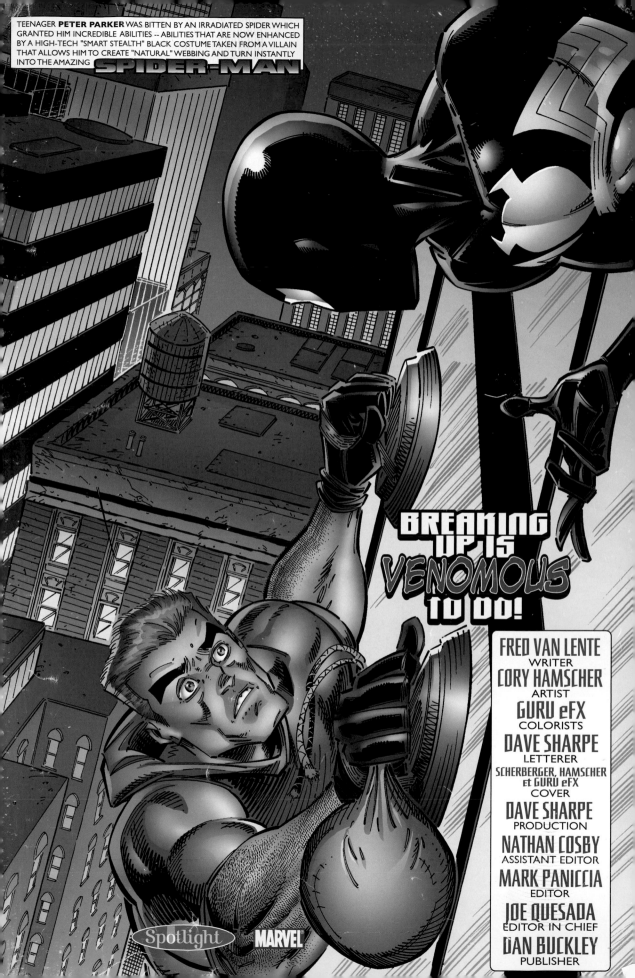

TEENAGER **PETER PARKER** WAS BITTEN BY AN IRRADIATED SPIDER WHICH GRANTED HIM INCREDIBLE ABILITIES -- ABILITIES THAT ARE NOW ENHANCED BY A HIGH-TECH "SMART STEALTH" BLACK COSTUME TAKEN FROM A VILLAIN THAT ALLOWS HIM TO CREATE "NATURAL" WEBBING AND TURN INSTANTLY INTO THE AMAZING **SPIDER-MAN**

BREAKING UP IS VENOMOUS TO DO!

FRED VAN LENTE
WRITER

CORY HAMSCHER
ARTIST

GURU eFX
COLORISTS

DAVE SHARPE
LETTERER

SCHERBERGER, HAMSCHER et GURU eFX
COVER

DAVE SHARPE
PRODUCTION

NATHAN COSBY
ASSISTANT EDITOR

MARK PANICCIA
EDITOR

JOE QUESADA
EDITOR IN CHIEF

DAN BUCKLEY
PUBLISHER

Spotlight   MARVEL

J
Graphic novel

VISIT US AT
www.abdopublishing.com

Reinforced library bound edition published in 2008 by Spotlight, a division of the ABDO Publishing Group, 8000 West 78th Street, Edina, Minnesota 55439. Spotlight produces high-quality reinforced library bound editions for schools and libraries. Published by agreement with Marvel Characters, Inc.

Library of Congress Cataloging-in-Publication Data

Van Lente, Fred.
Breaking up is venomous to do! / Fred Van Lente, writer ; Cory Hamscher, artist ; GURU eFX, colorists ; Dave Sharpe, letterer. -- Reinforced library bound ed.
p. cm. -- (Spider-man)
"Marvel age"--Cover.
Revision of issue 24 of Marvel adventures Spider-man.
ISBN 978-1-59961-393-2
1. Graphic novels. I. Hamscher, Cory. II. Marvel adventures. Spider-man. 24. III. Title.

PN6728.S6V34 2008
741.5'973--dc22

2007020252

Spotlight

All Spotlight books have reinforced library bindings and are manufactured in the United States of America.

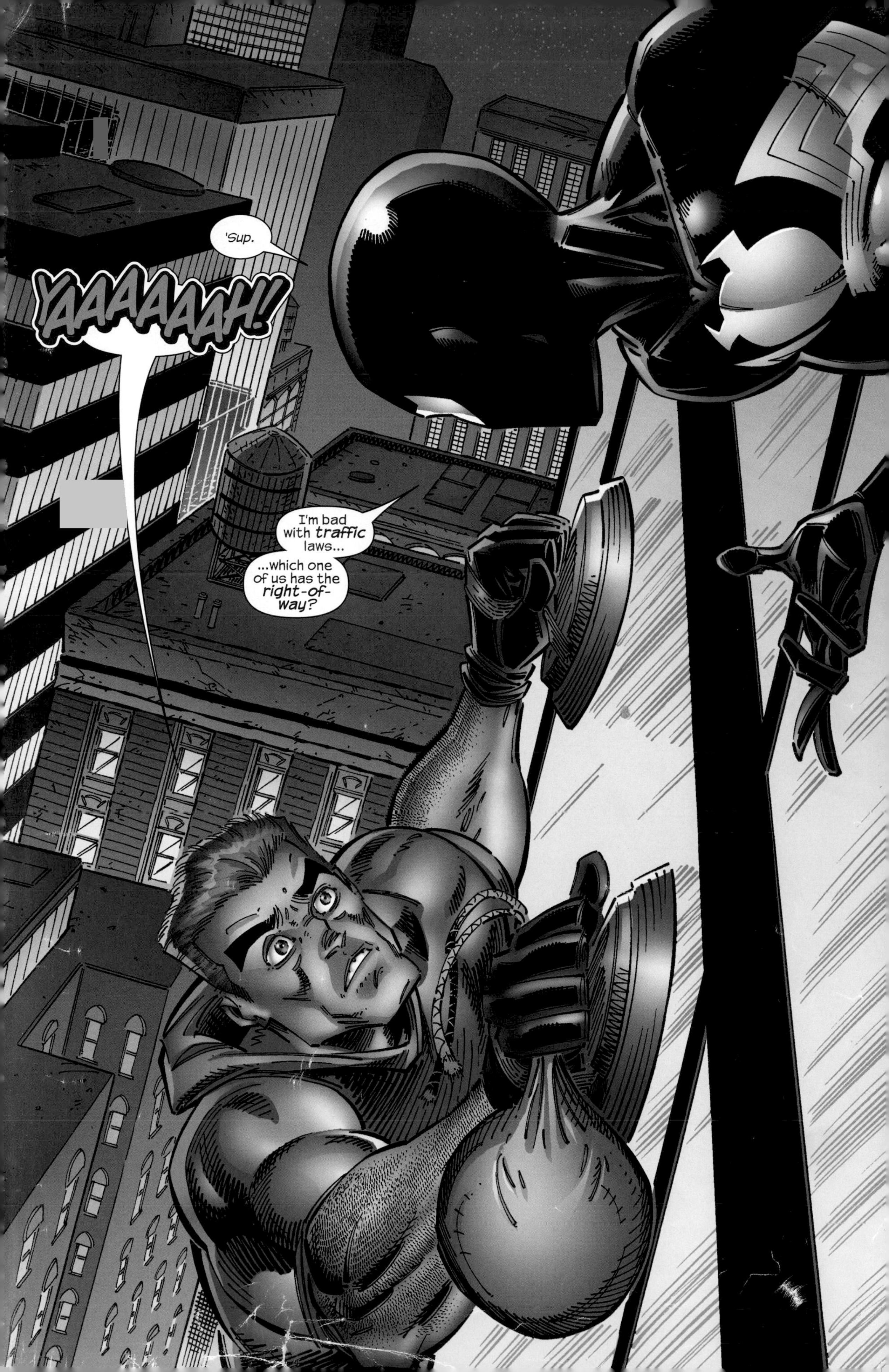
'Sup.
YAAAAAAH!
I'm bad with traffic laws...
...which one of us has the right-of-way?

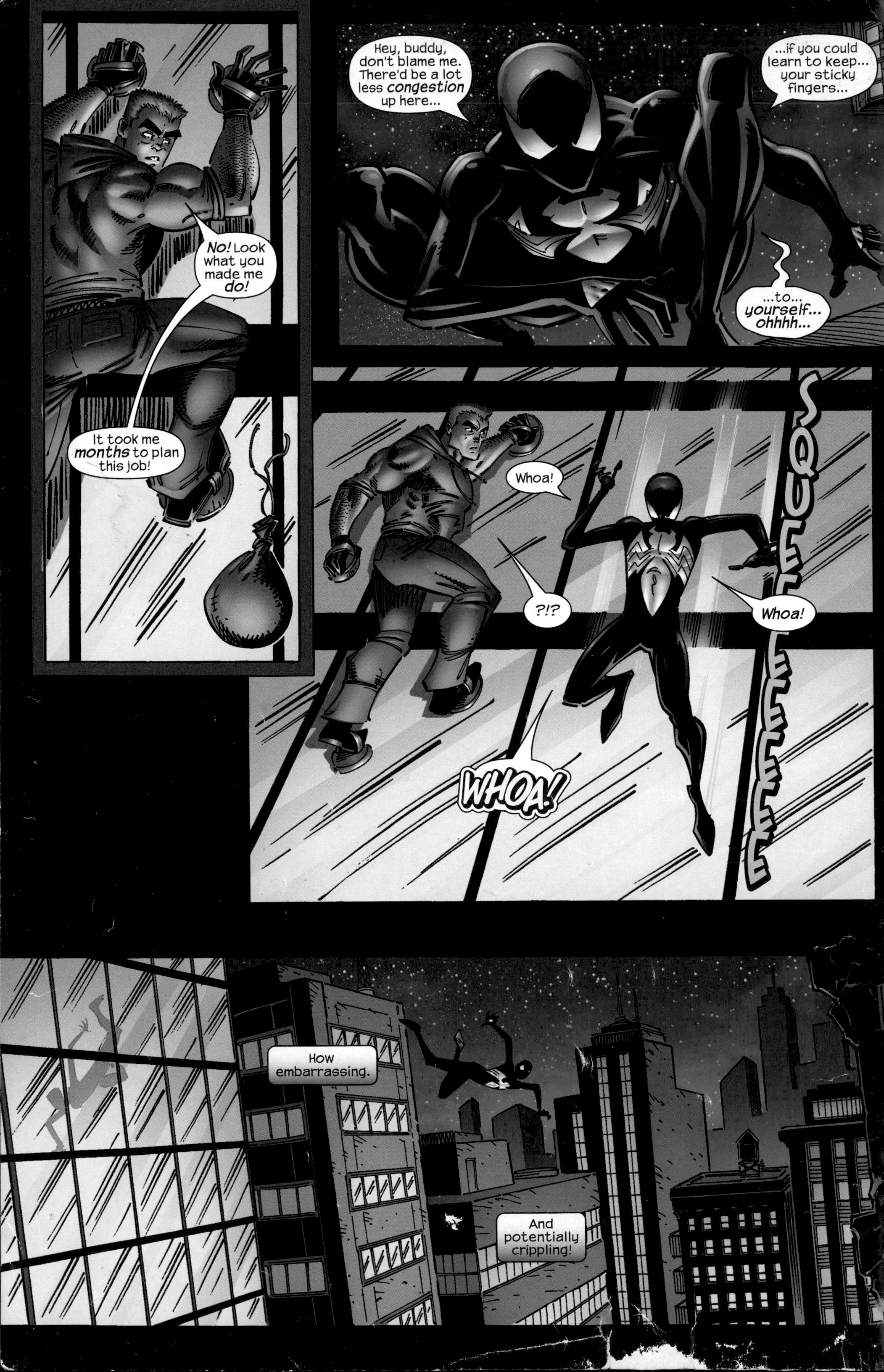
No! Look what you made me do!
It took me months to plan this job!
Hey, buddy, don't blame me. There'd be a lot less congestion up here...
...if you could learn to keep... your sticky fingers...
...to... yourself... ohhhh...
Whoa!
?!?
Whoa!
WHOA!
SQUEEEEEEEEE
How embarrassing.
And potentially crippling!

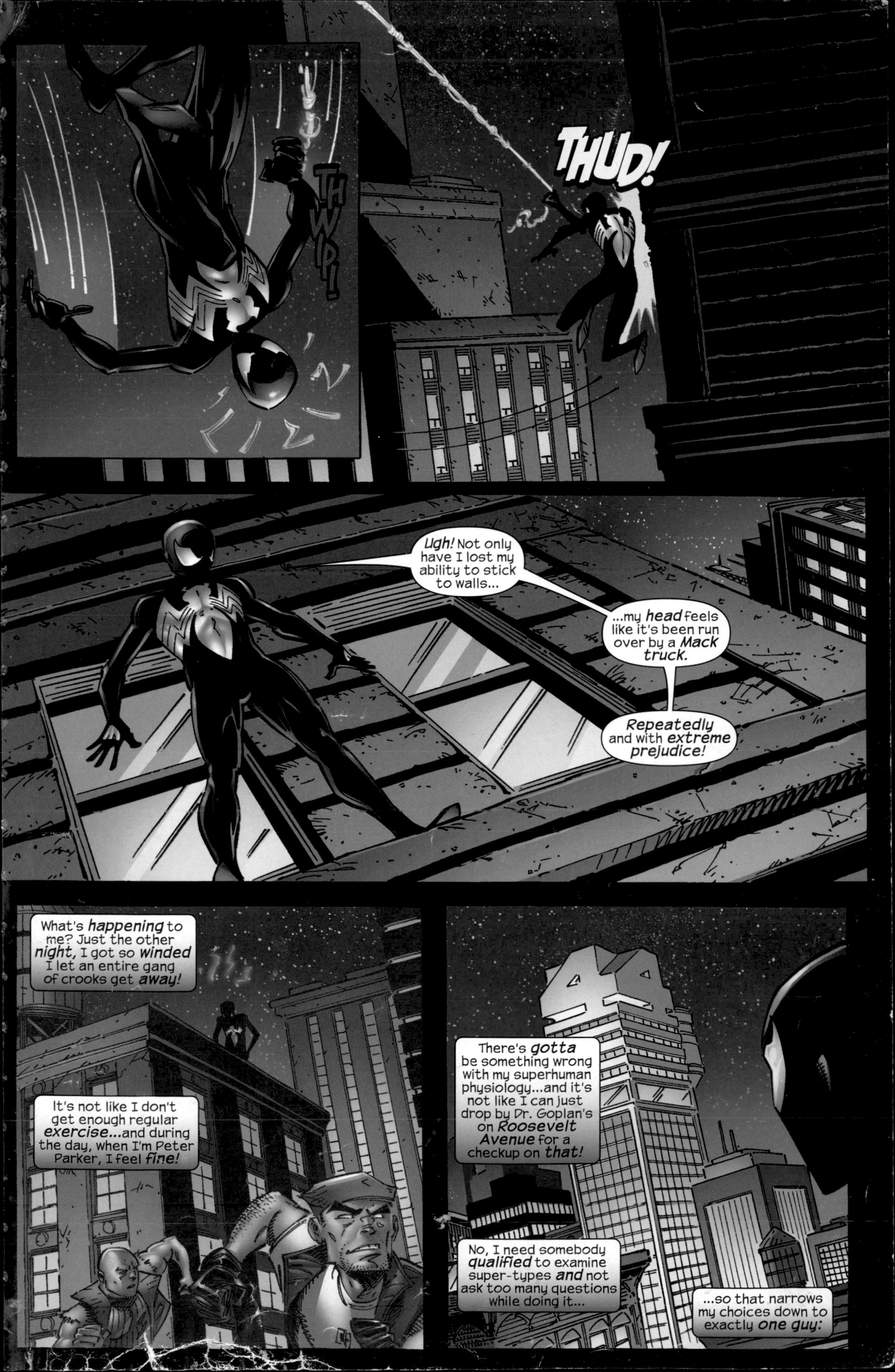
THWIP!
THUD!
Ugh! Not only have I lost my ability to stick to walls...
...my head feels like it's been run over by a Mack truck.
Repeatedly and with extreme prejudice!
What's happening to me? Just the other night, I got so winded I let an entire gang of crooks get away!
It's not like I don't get enough regular exercise...and during the day, when I'm Peter Parker, I feel fine!
There's gotta be something wrong with my superhuman physiology...and it's not like I can just drop by Dr. Goplan's on Roosevelt Avenue for a checkup on that!
No, I need somebody qualified to examine super-types and not ask too many questions while doing it...
...so that narrows my choices down to exactly one guy:

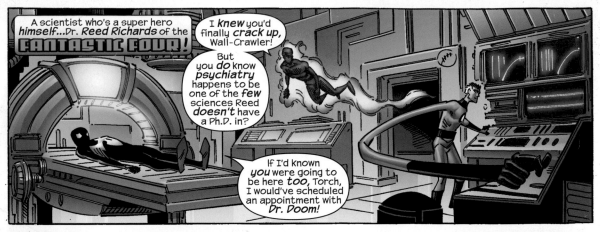

A scientist who's a super hero *himself*...Dr. *Reed Richards* of the **FANTASTIC FOUR!**

I *knew* you'd finally *crack up*, Wall-Crawler!

But you *do* know psychiatry happens to be one of the *few* sciences Reed *doesn't* have a Ph.D. in?

If I'd known *you* were going to be here *too*, Torch, I would've scheduled an appointment with *Dr. Doom!*

Hmmm...though all my instruments appear properly *calibrated*...

...they're picking up *two* life readings off you, Spider-Man! How can that be *accurate?*

Unless...

...this *new costume* you're wearing. You say it's made of a *"smart stealth"* material that can read your surface thoughts-- move on and off of you under its *own power*--and form "natural webbing" out of itself?

Yeah! It's the *greatest!*

Hmmm... that may very well *be*...

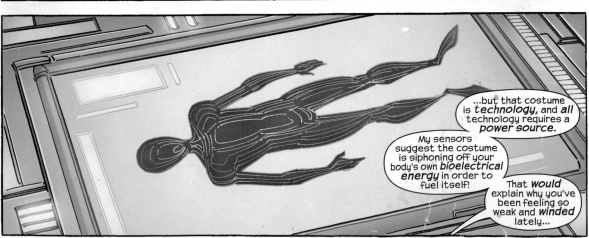

...but that costume is *technology*, and *all* technology requires a *power source.*

My sensors suggest the costume is siphoning off your body's own *bioelectrical energy* in order to fuel itself!

That *would* explain why you've been feeling so *weak* and *winded* lately...

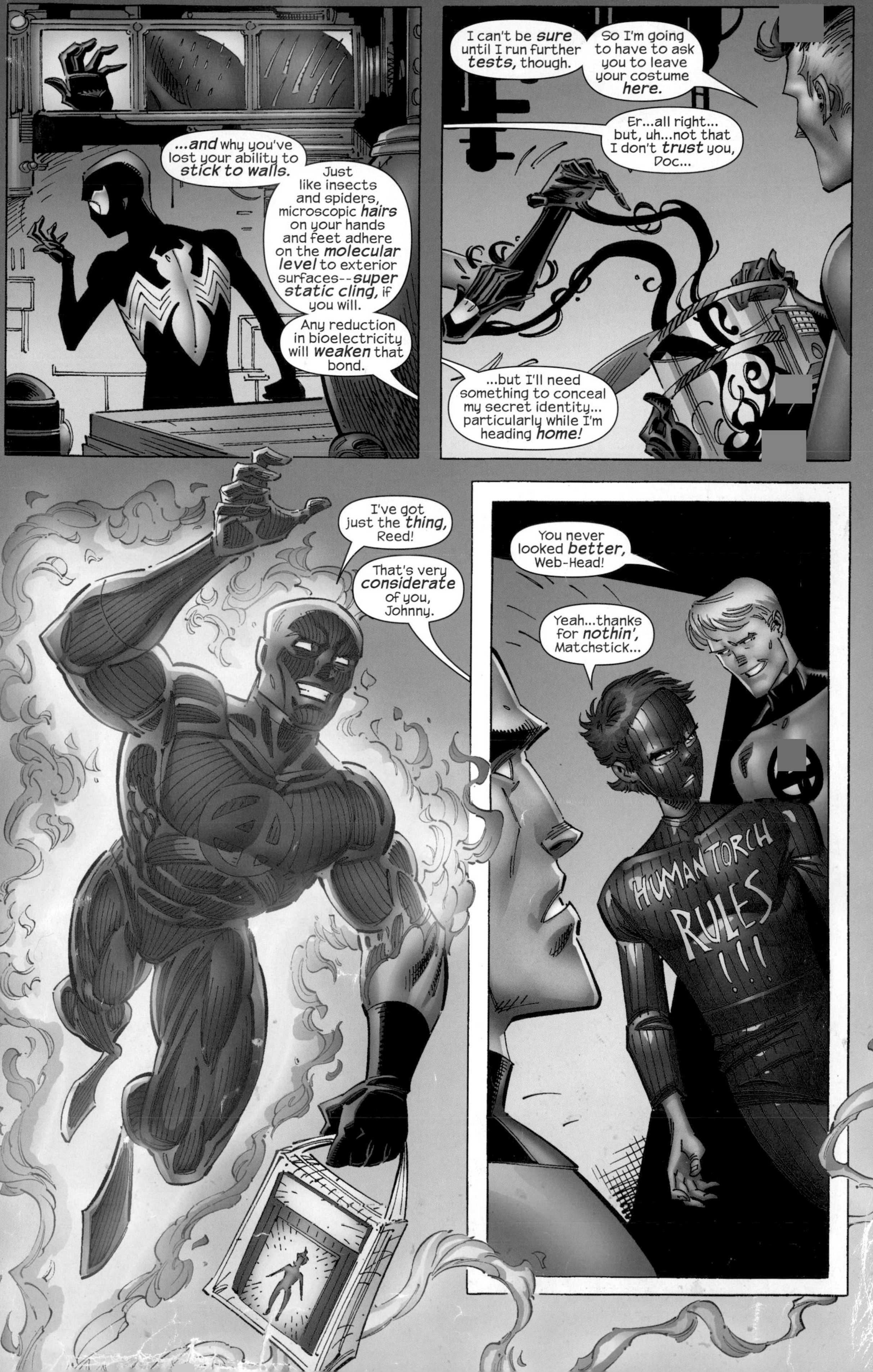
...and why you've lost your ability to stick to walls.
Just like insects and spiders, microscopic hairs on your hands and feet adhere on the molecular level to exterior surfaces--super static cling, if you will.
Any reduction in bioelectricity will weaken that bond.
I can't be sure until I run further tests, though.
So I'm going to have to ask you to leave your costume here.
Er...all right... but, uh...not that I don't trust you, Doc...
...but I'll need something to conceal my secret identity... particularly while I'm heading home!
I've got just the thing, Reed!
That's very considerate of you, Johnny.
You never looked better, Web-Head!
Yeah...thanks for nothin', Matchstick...
HUMAN TORCH RULES !!!

Later that night, in Fantastic Four Headquarters...

Heh, heh!

The perfect *crime!*

"Maybe the *Wall-Crawler* can't handle this super-suit...

"...but I would look *so sweet* in *black* I can barely *stand* it!"

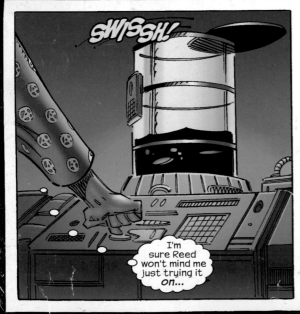

SWISSH!

I'm sure Reed won't mind me just trying it *on...*

Gross!

It's...like... *tingly!*

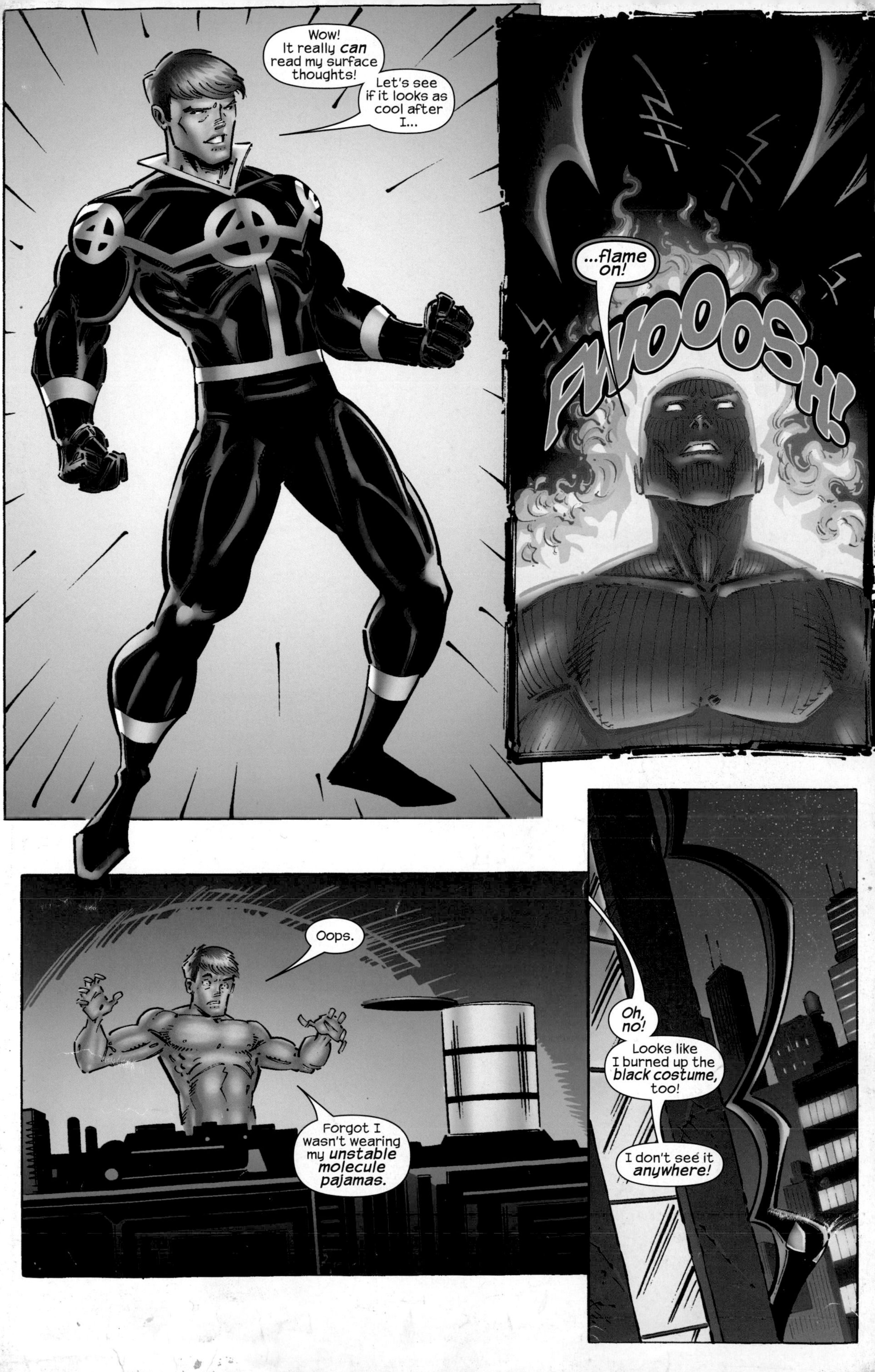

Wow! It really can read my surface thoughts!
Let's see if it looks as cool after I...
...flame on!
FWOOOOSH!
Oops.
Forgot I wasn't wearing my unstable molecule pajamas.
Oh, no!
Looks like I burned up the black costume, too!
I don't see it anywhere!

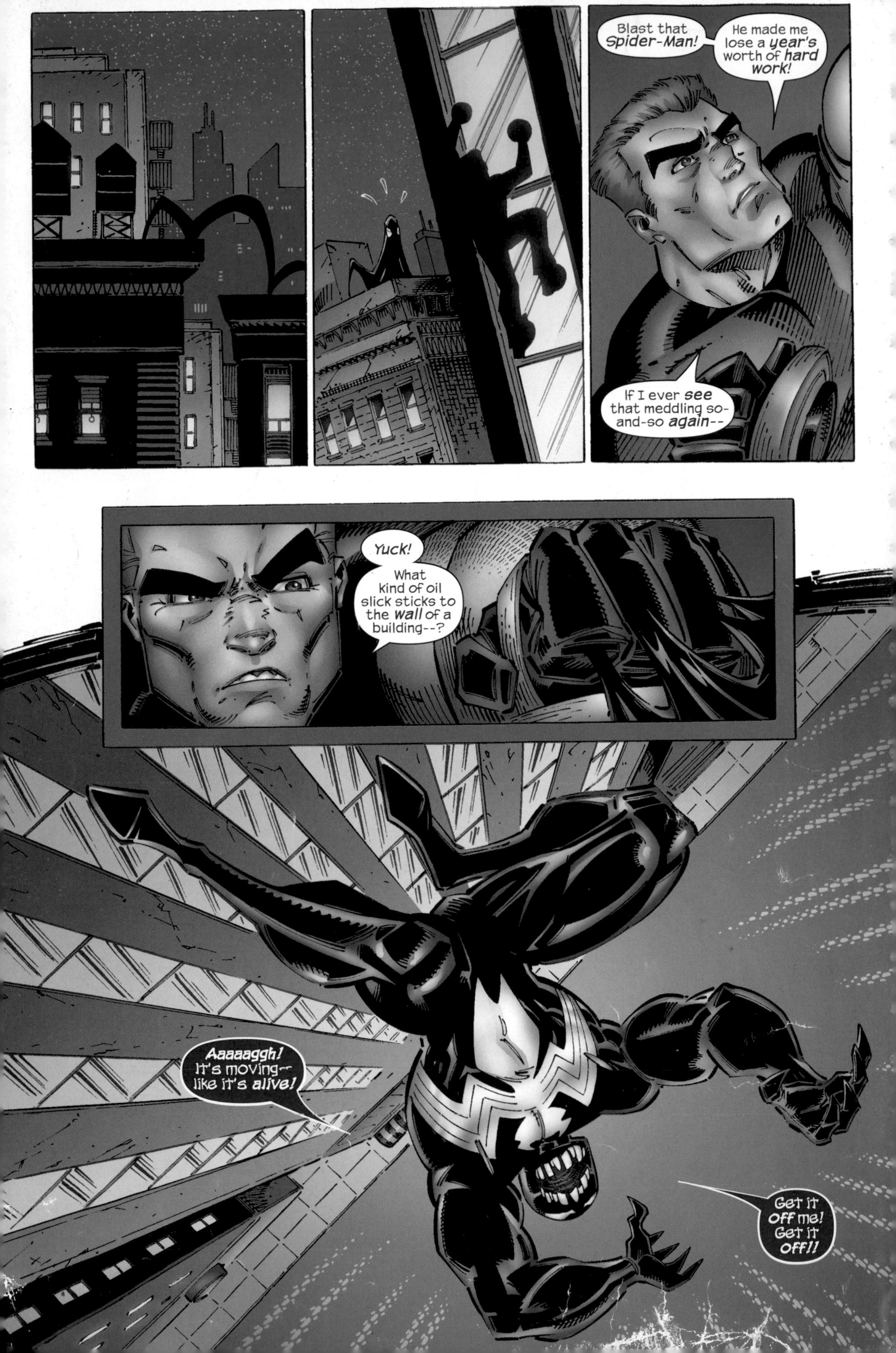
Blast that Spider-Man!
He made me lose a year's worth of hard work!
If I ever see that meddling so-and-so again--
Yuck!
What kind of oil slick sticks to the wall of a building--?
Aaaaaggh! It's moving--like it's alive!
Get it off me! Get it off!!

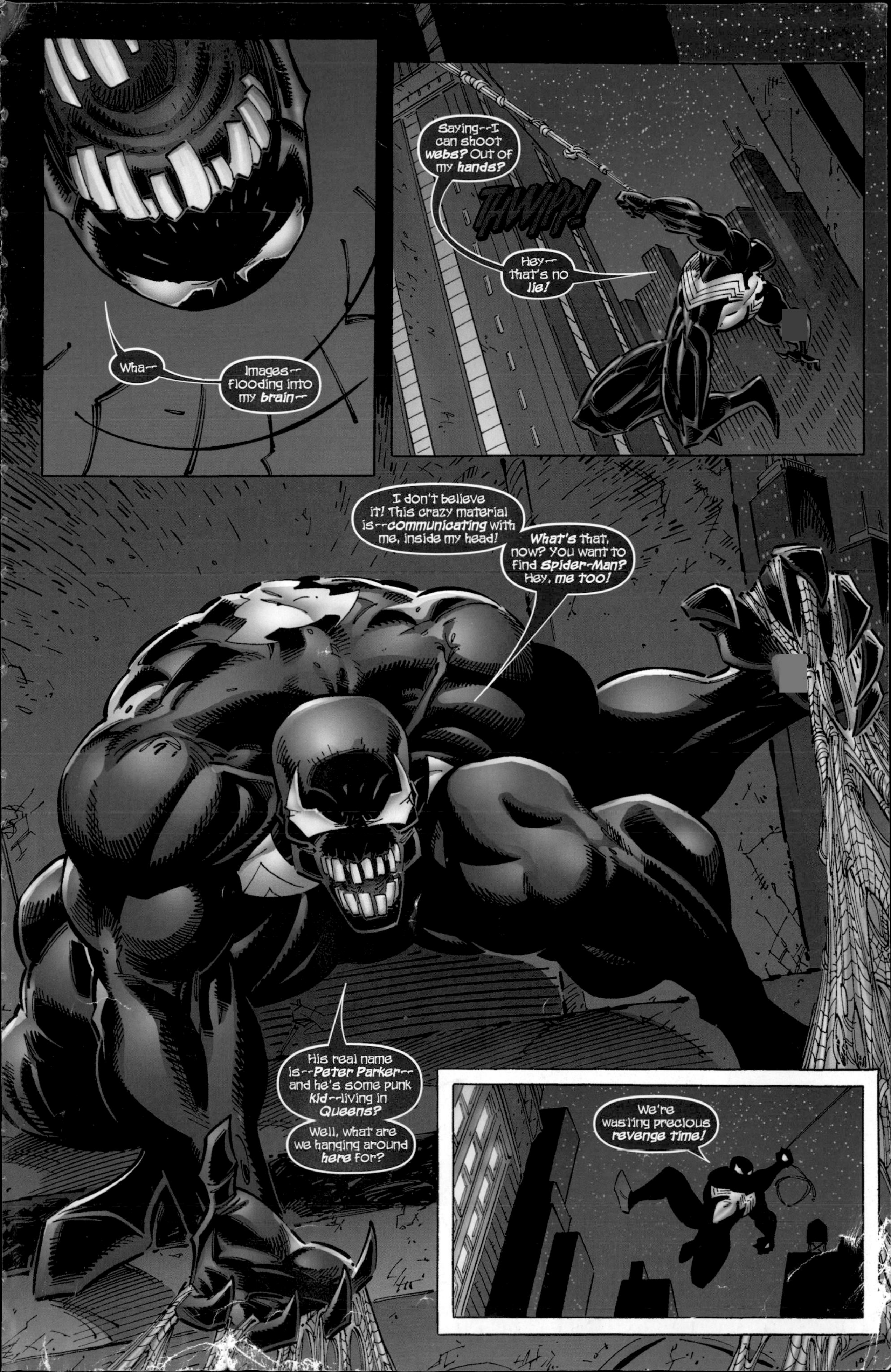
Wha--
Images--flooding into my brain--
Saying--I can shoot webs? Out of my hands?
THWIPP!
Hey--that's no lie!
I don't believe it! This crazy material is--communicating with me, inside my head!
What's that, now? You want to find Spider-Man? Hey, me too!
His real name is--Peter Parker--and he's some punk kid--living in Queens?
Well, what are we hanging around here for?
We're wasting precious revenge time!

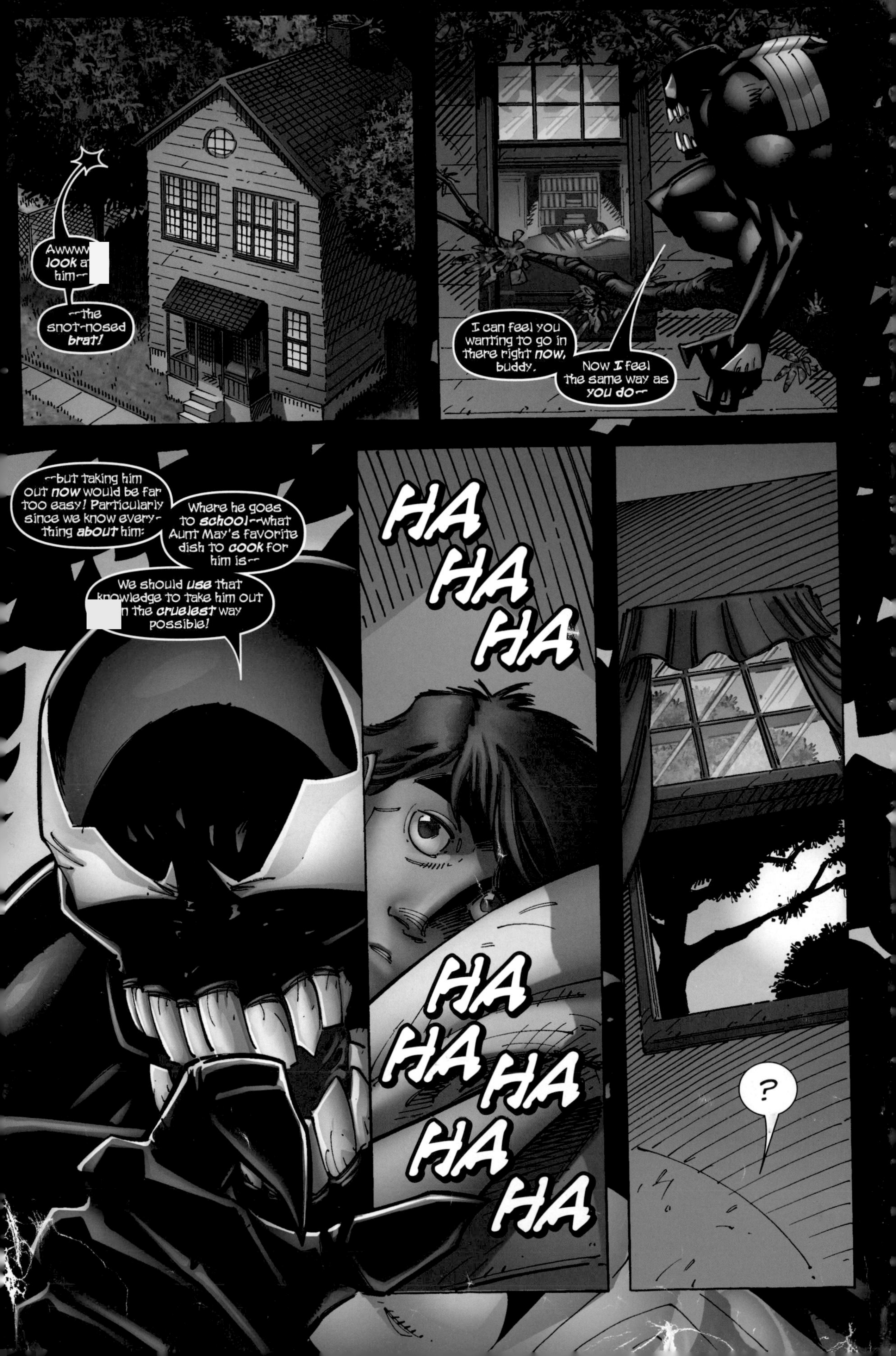
Awwww look a him--
--the snot-nosed brat!
I can feel you wanting to go in there right now, buddy.
Now I feel the same way as you do--
--but taking him out now would be far too easy! Particularly since we know everything about him:
Where he goes to school--what Aunt May's favorite dish to cook for him is--
We should use that knowledge to take him out n the cruelest way possible!
HA HA HA
HA HA HA HA HA
?

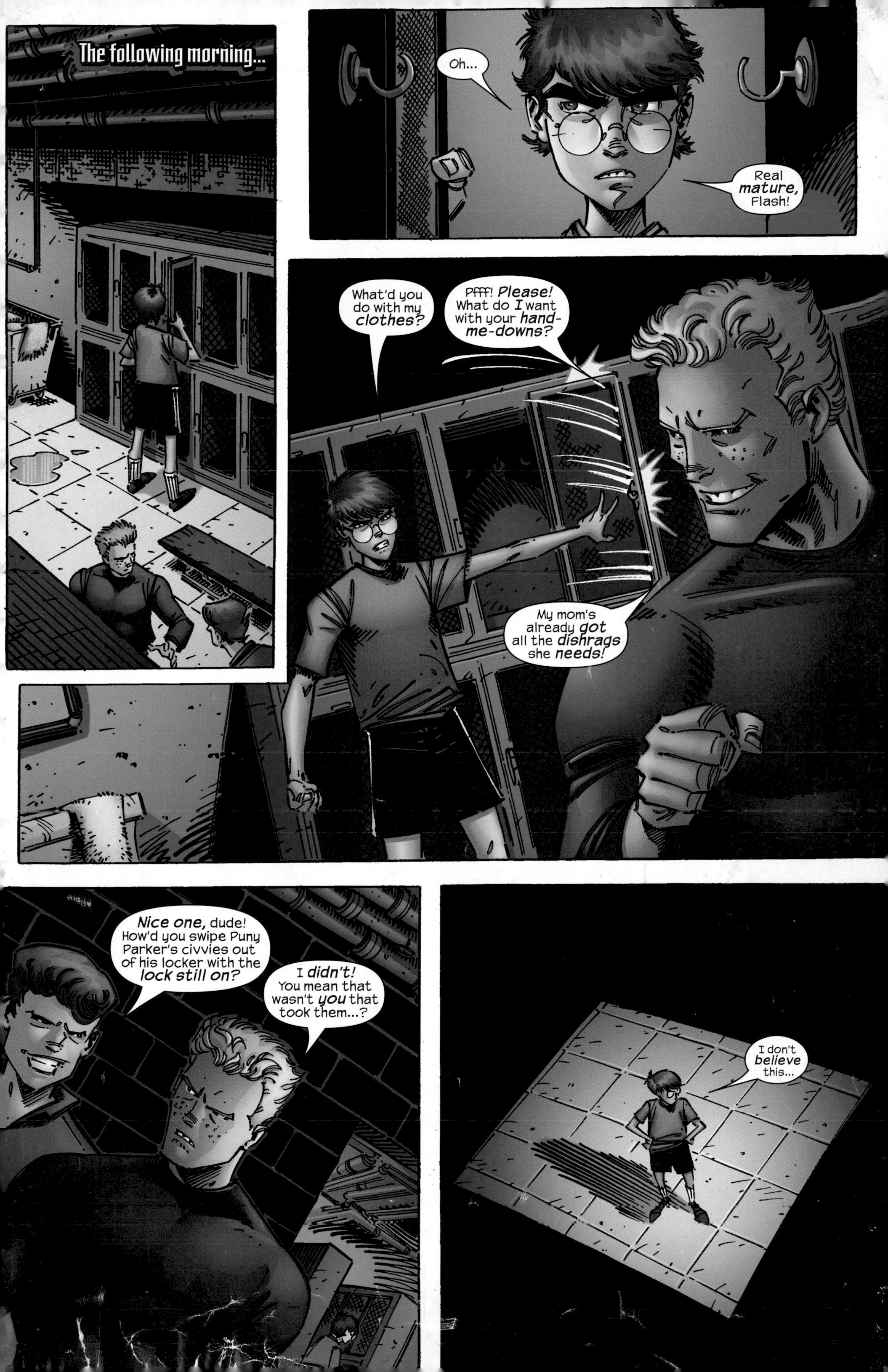
The following morning...
Oh...
Real mature, Flash!
What'd you do with my clothes?
Pfff! Please! What do I want with your hand-me-downs?
My mom's already got all the dishrags she needs!
Nice one, dude! How'd you swipe Puny Parker's civvies out of his locker with the lock still on?
I didn't! You mean that wasn't you that took them...?
I don't believe this...

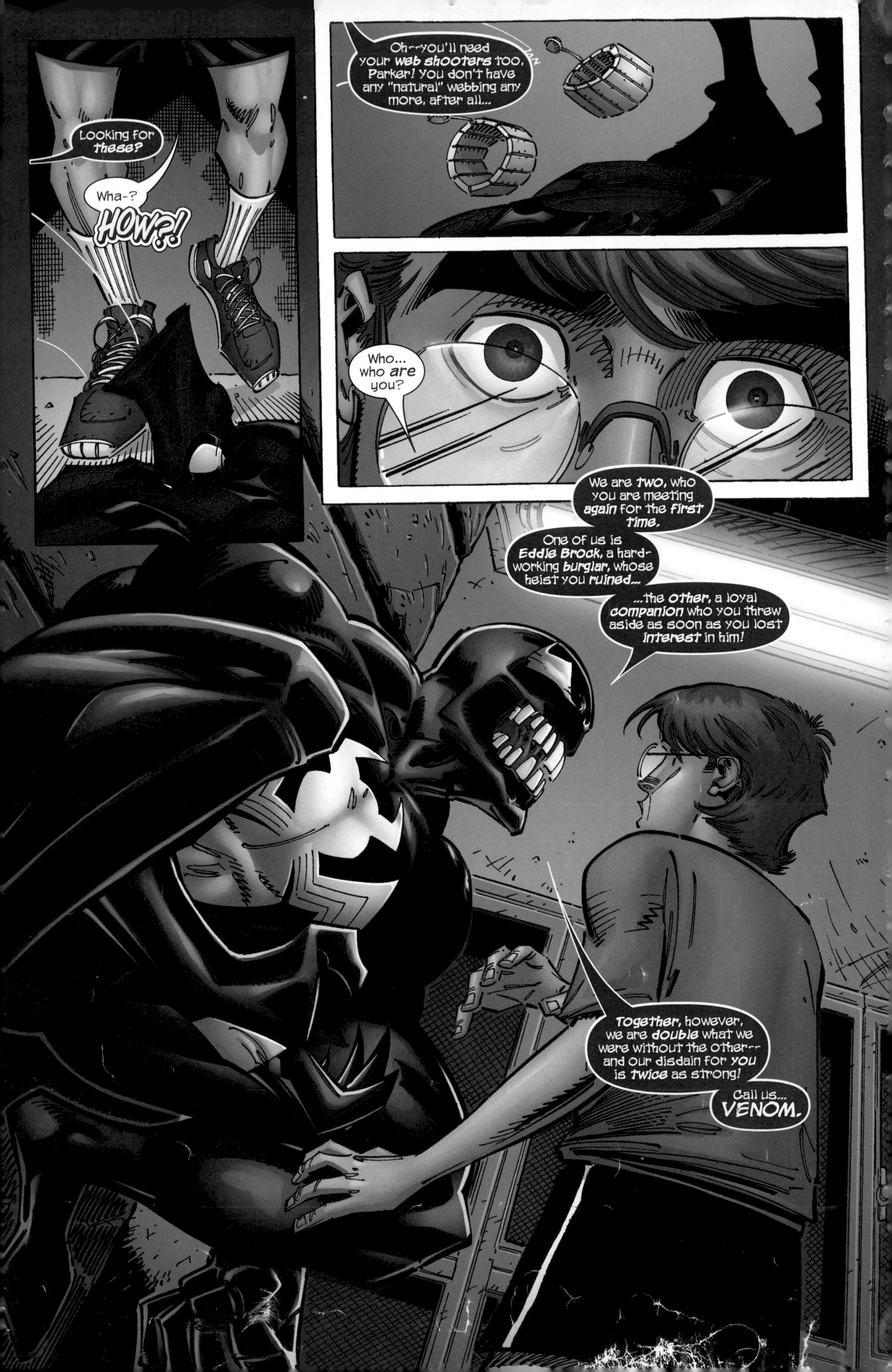
Looking for these?
Wha-?
HOW?!
Oh--you'll need your web shooters too, Parker! You don't have any "natural" webbing any more, after all...
Who... who are you?
We are two, who you are meeting again for the first time.
One of us is Eddie Brock, a hard-working burglar, whose heist you ruined...
...the other, a loyal companion who you threw aside as soon as you lost interest in him!
Together, however, we are double what we were without the other-- and our disdain for you is twice as strong!
Call us... VENOM.

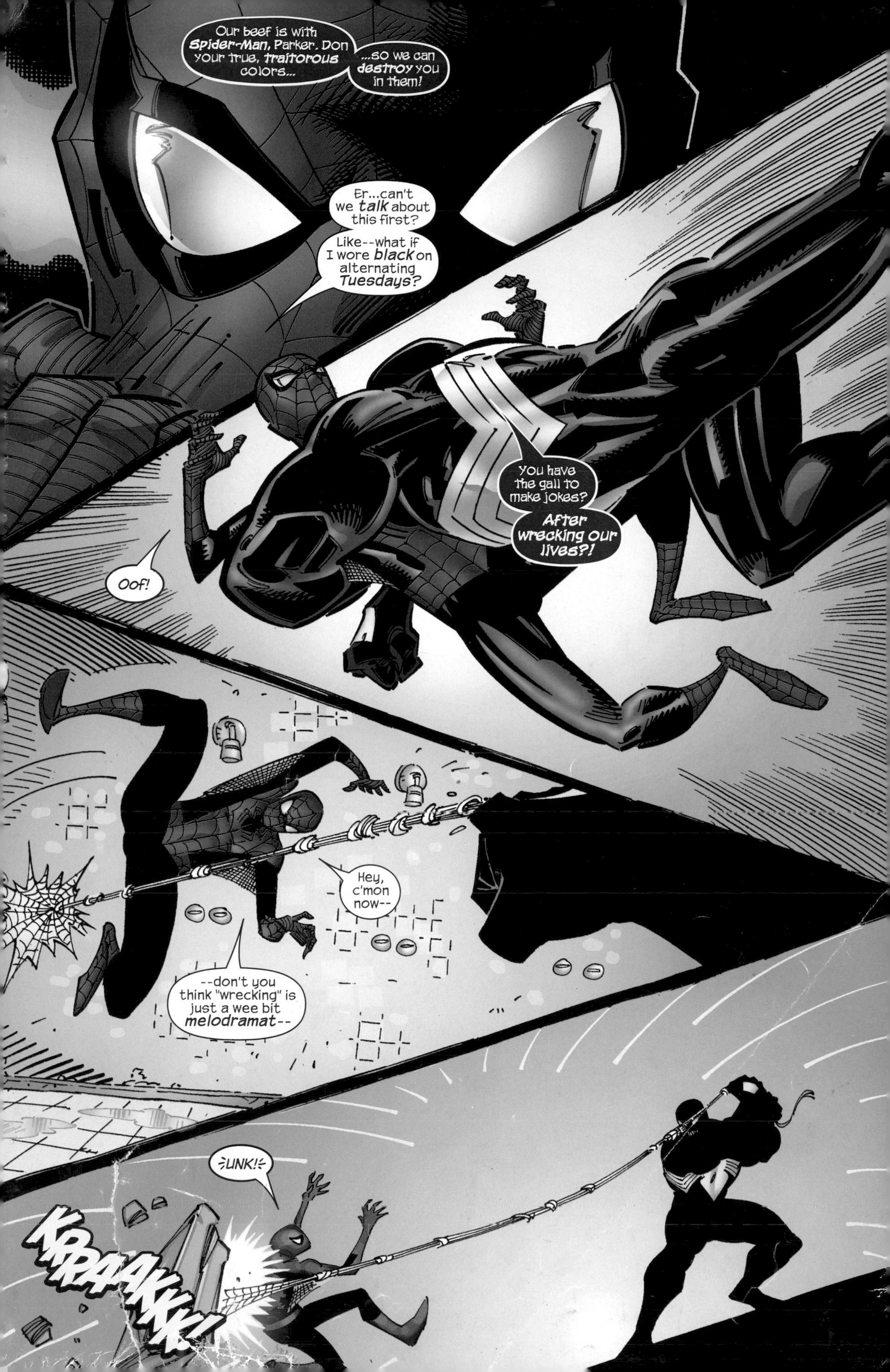
Our beef is with Spider-Man, Parker. Don your true, traitorous colors...
...so we can destroy you in them!
Er...can't we talk about this first?
Like--what if I wore black on alternating Tuesdays?
You have the gall to make jokes?
After wrecking our lives?!
Oof!
Hey, c'mon now--
--don't you think "wrecking" is just a wee bit melodramat--
UNK!
KRRAAKKK!

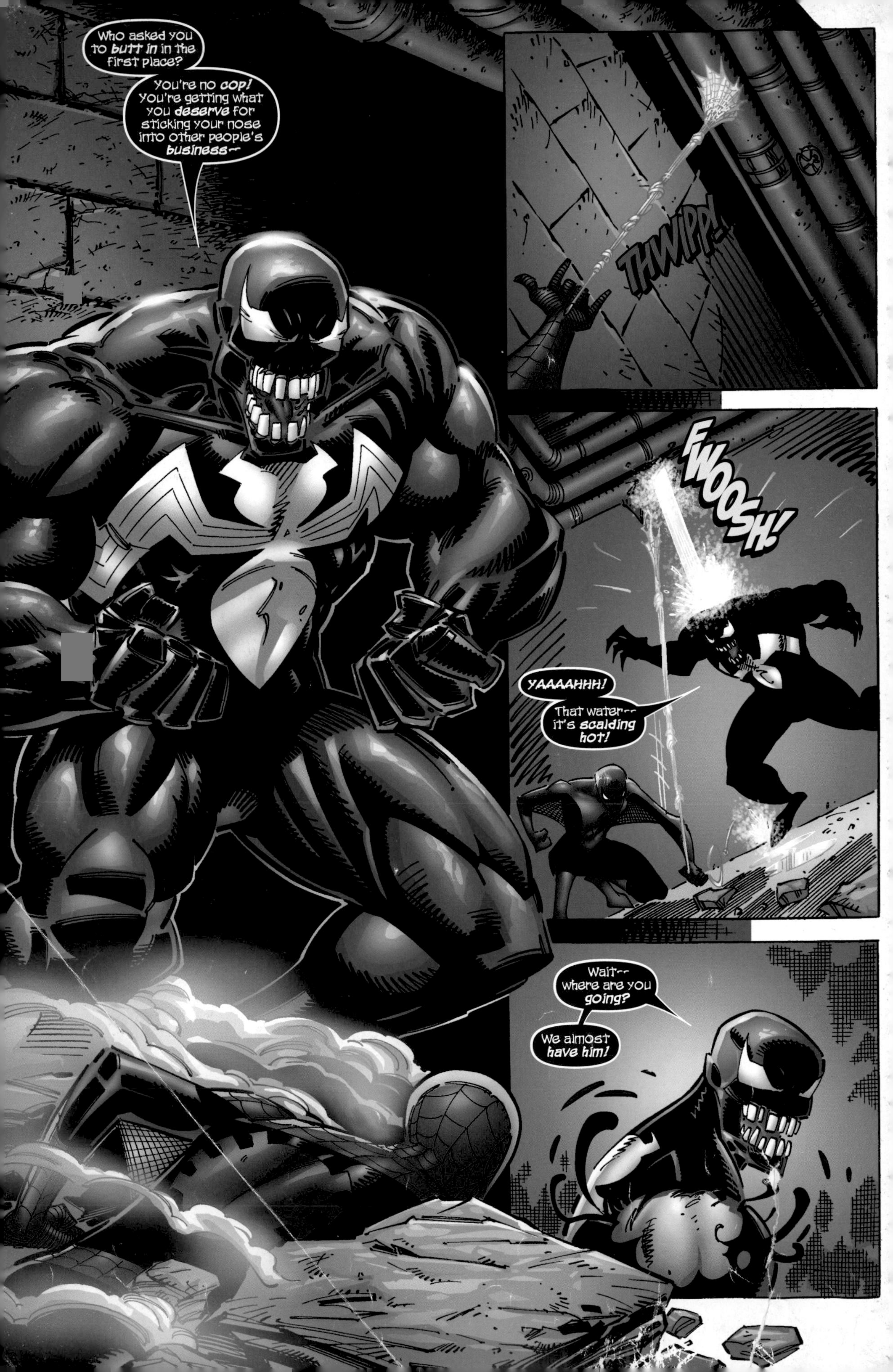
Who asked you to butt in in the first place?
You're no cop! You're getting what you deserve for sticking your nose into other people's business--
THWIPP!
FWOOSH!
YAAAAHHH!
That water-- it's scalding hot!
Wait-- where are you going?
We almost have him!

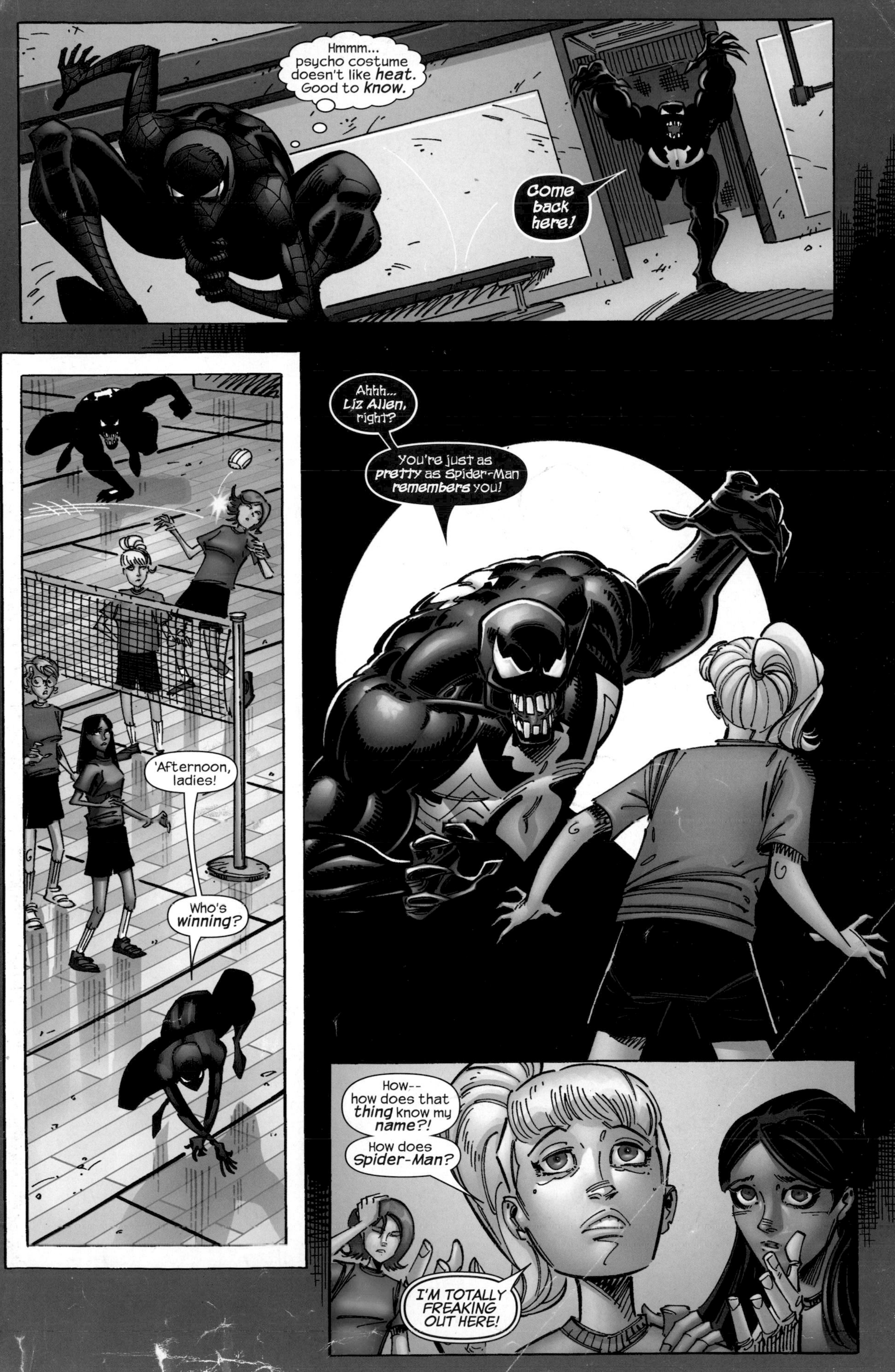

Hmmm... psycho costume doesn't like heat. Good to know.
Come back here!
'Afternoon, ladies!
Who's winning?
Ahhh... Liz Allen, right?
You're just as pretty as Spider-Man remembers you!
How-- how does that thing know my name?!
How does Spider-Man?
I'M TOTALLY FREAKING OUT HERE!

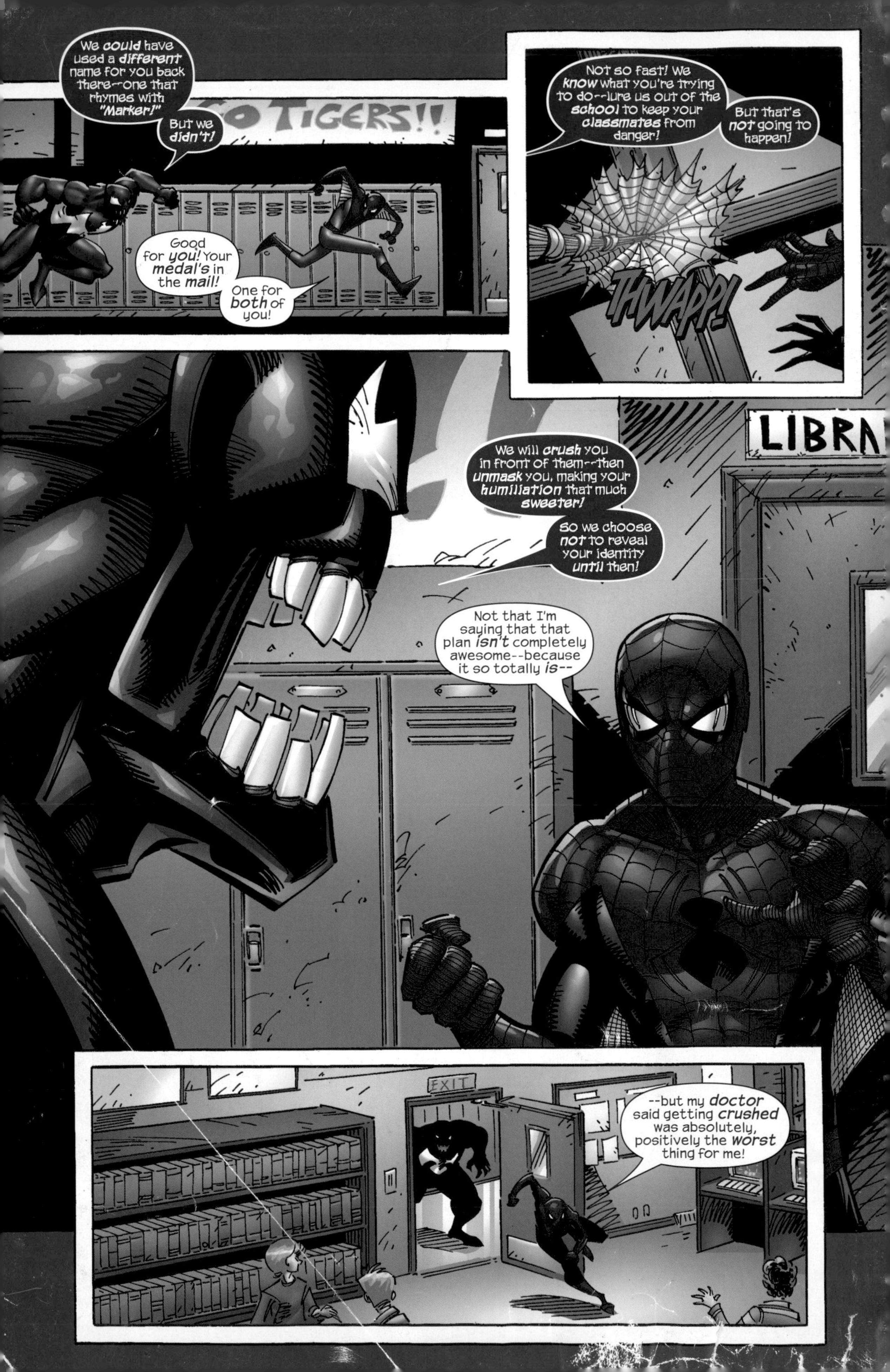
We could have used a different name for you back there--one that rhymes with "Marker!"
But we didn't!
Good for you! Your medal's in the mail!
One for both of you!
GO TIGERS!!
Not so fast! We know what you're trying to do--lure us out of the school to keep your classmates from danger!
But that's not going to happen!
THWAPP!
LIBRA
We will crush you in front of them--then unmask you, making your humiliation that much sweeter!
So we choose not to reveal your identity until then!
Not that I'm saying that that plan isn't completely awesome--because it so totally is--
EXIT
--but my doctor said getting crushed was absolutely, positively the worst thing for me!

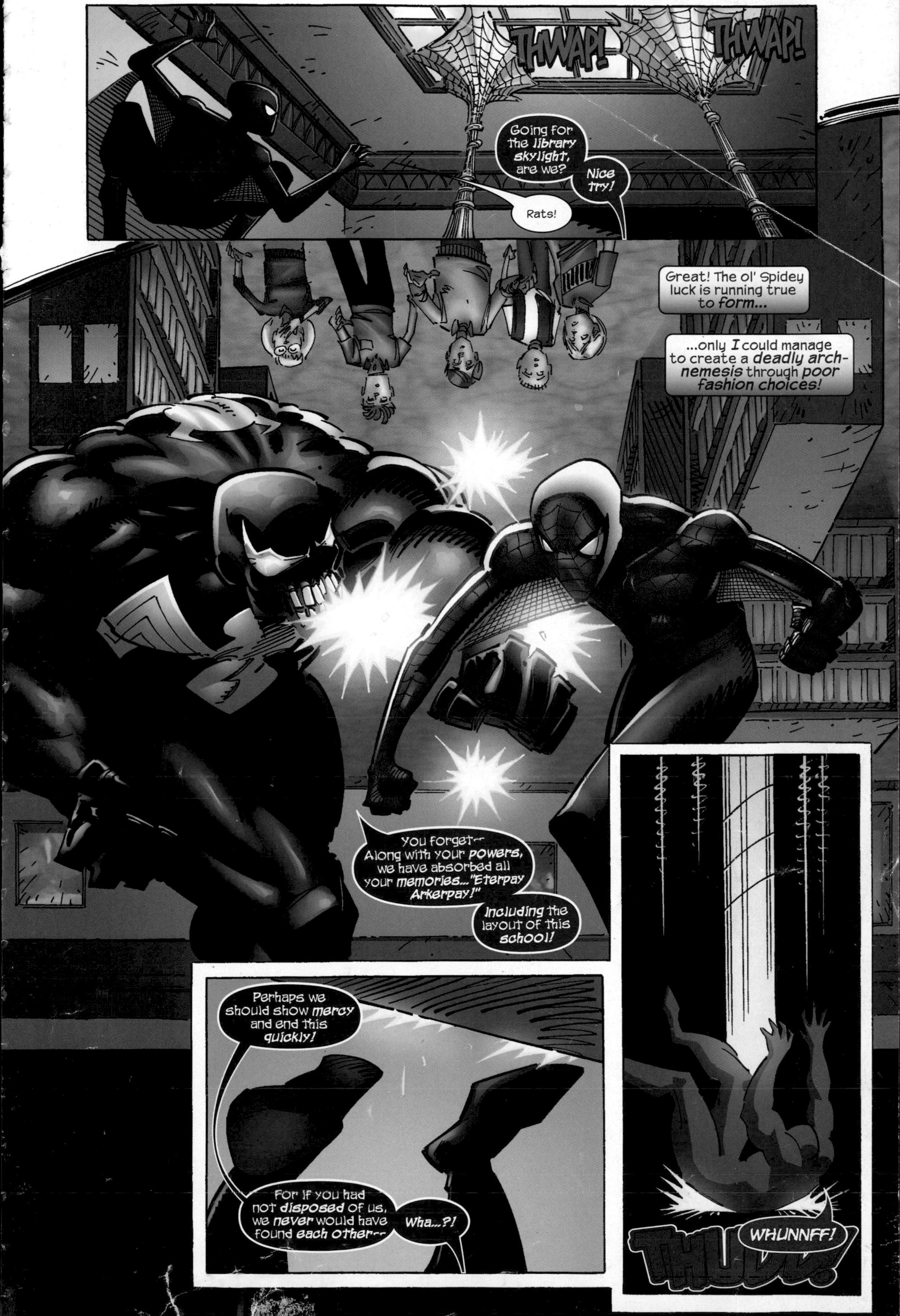
THWAP!
THWAP!
Going for the library skylight, are we?
Nice try!
Rats!
Great! The ol' Spidey luck is running true to form...
...only I could manage to create a deadly arch-nemesis through poor fashion choices!
You forget-- Along with your powers, we have absorbed all your memories... "Eterpay Arkerpay!"
Including the layout of this school!
Perhaps we should show mercy and end this quickly!
For if you had not disposed of us, we never would have found each other--
Wha...?!
WHUNNFF!
THUDD!

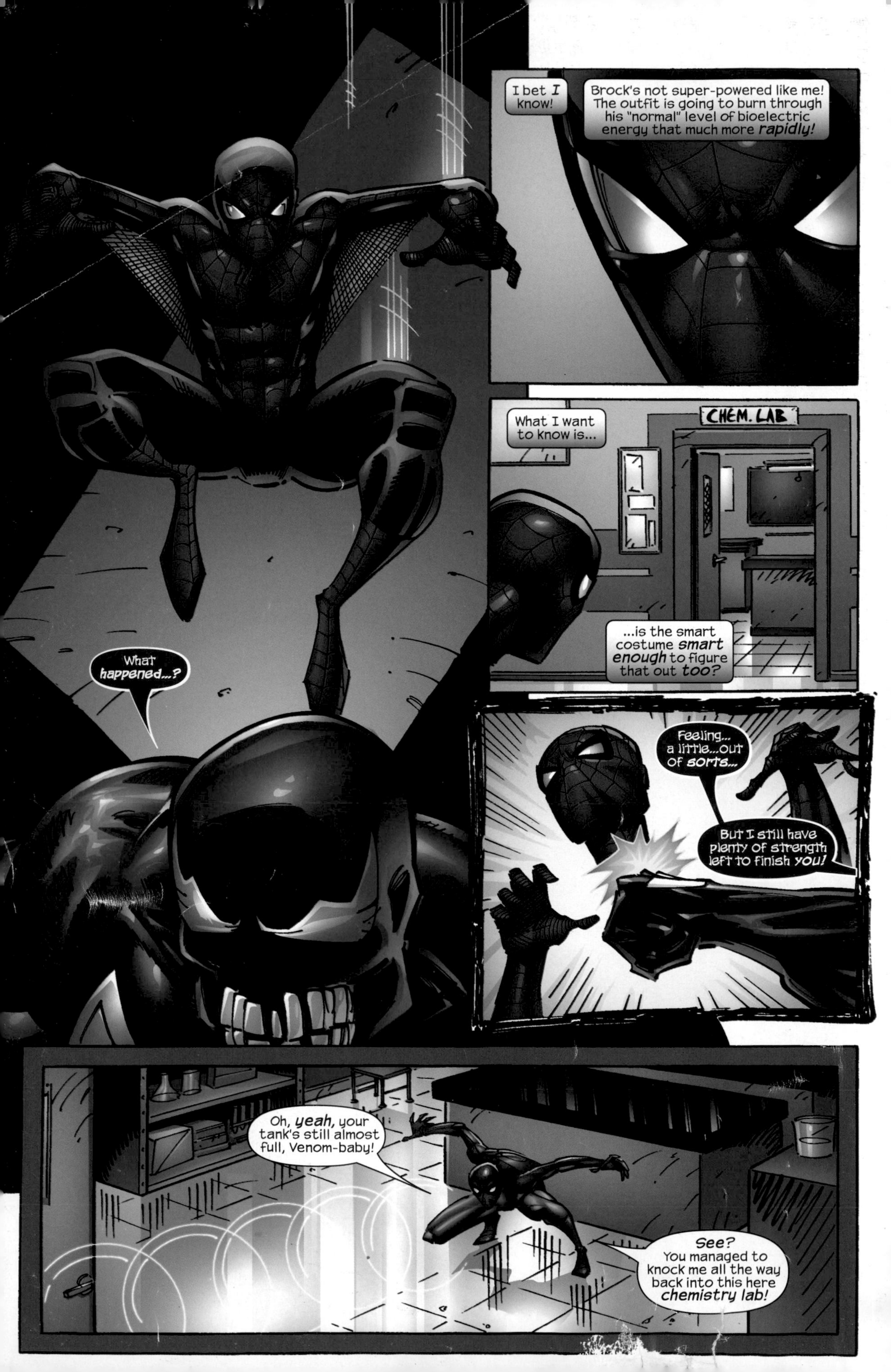
What happened...?
I bet I know!
Brock's not super-powered like me! The outfit is going to burn through his "normal" level of bioelectric energy that much more rapidly!
What I want to know is...
CHEM. LAB
...is the smart costume smart enough to figure that out too?
Feeling... a little...out of sorts...
But I still have plenty of strength left to finish you!
Oh, yeah, your tank's still almost full, Venom-baby!
See? You managed to knock me all the way back into this here chemistry lab!

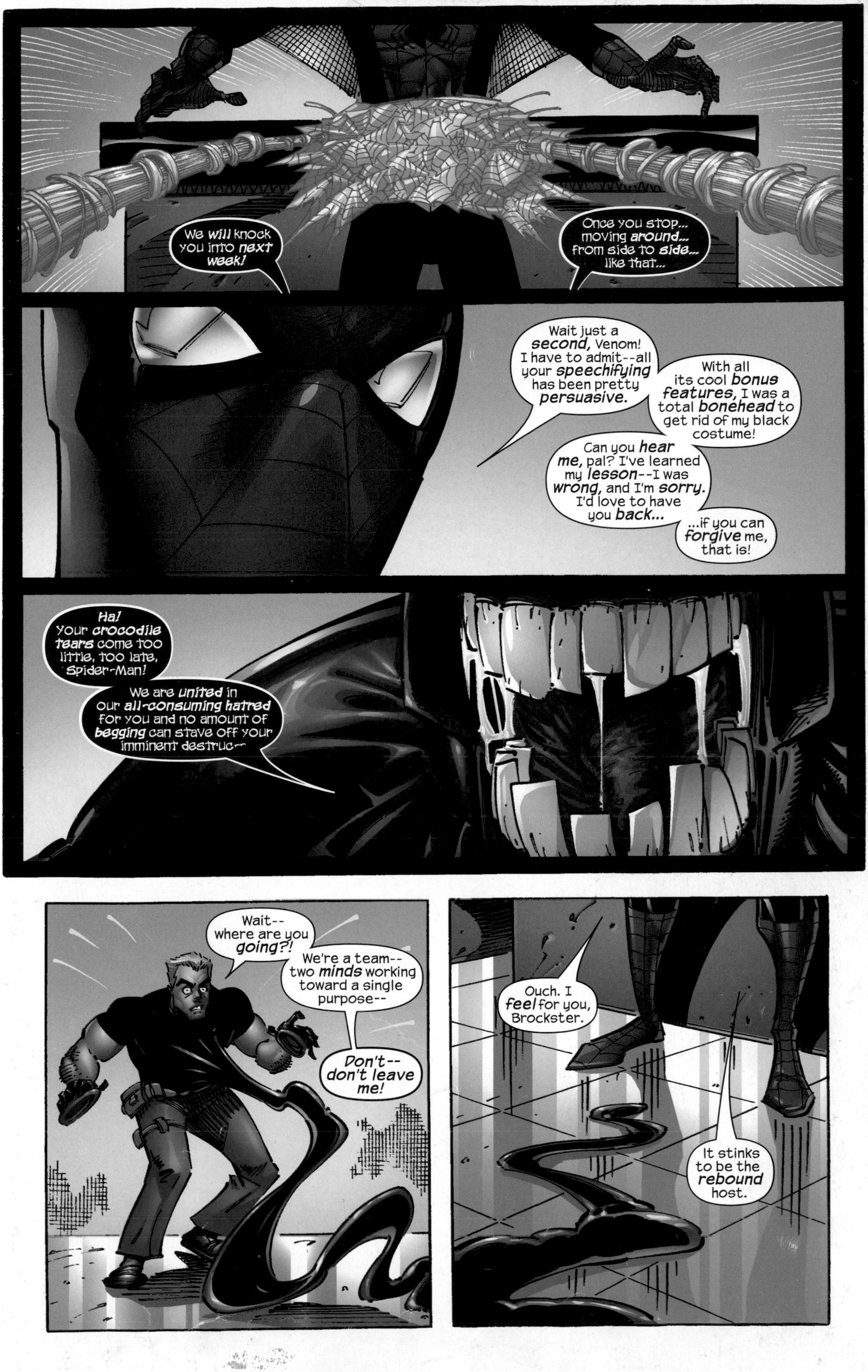

We will knock you into next week!
Once you stop... moving around... from side to side... like that...
Wait just a second, Venom! I have to admit--all your speechifying has been pretty persuasive.
With all its cool bonus features, I was a total bonehead to get rid of my black costume!
Can you hear me, pal? I've learned my lesson--I was wrong, and I'm sorry. I'd love to have you back...
...if you can forgive me, that is!
Ha! Your crocodile tears come too little, too late, Spider-Man!
We are united in our all-consuming hatred for you and no amount of begging can stave off your imminent destruc--
Wait-- where are you going?!
We're a team-- two minds working toward a single purpose--
Don't-- don't leave me!
Ouch. I feel for you, Brockster.
It stinks to be the rebound host.

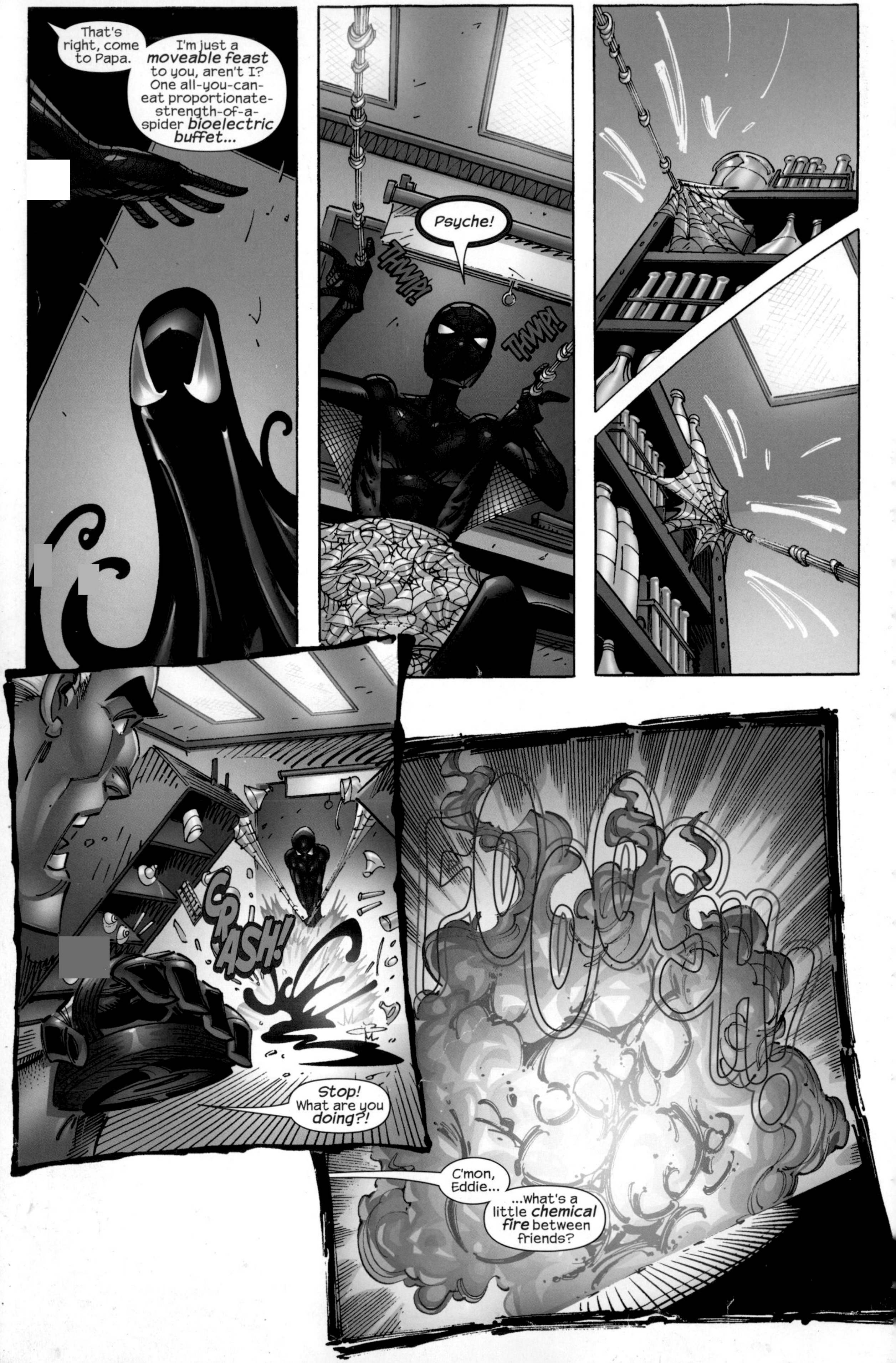
That's right, come to Papa.
I'm just a moveable feast to you, aren't I? One all-you-can-eat proportionate-strength-of-a-spider bioelectric buffet...
Psyche!
THWP!
THWP!
CRASH!
Stop! What are you doing?!
C'mon, Eddie...
...what's a little chemical fire between friends?

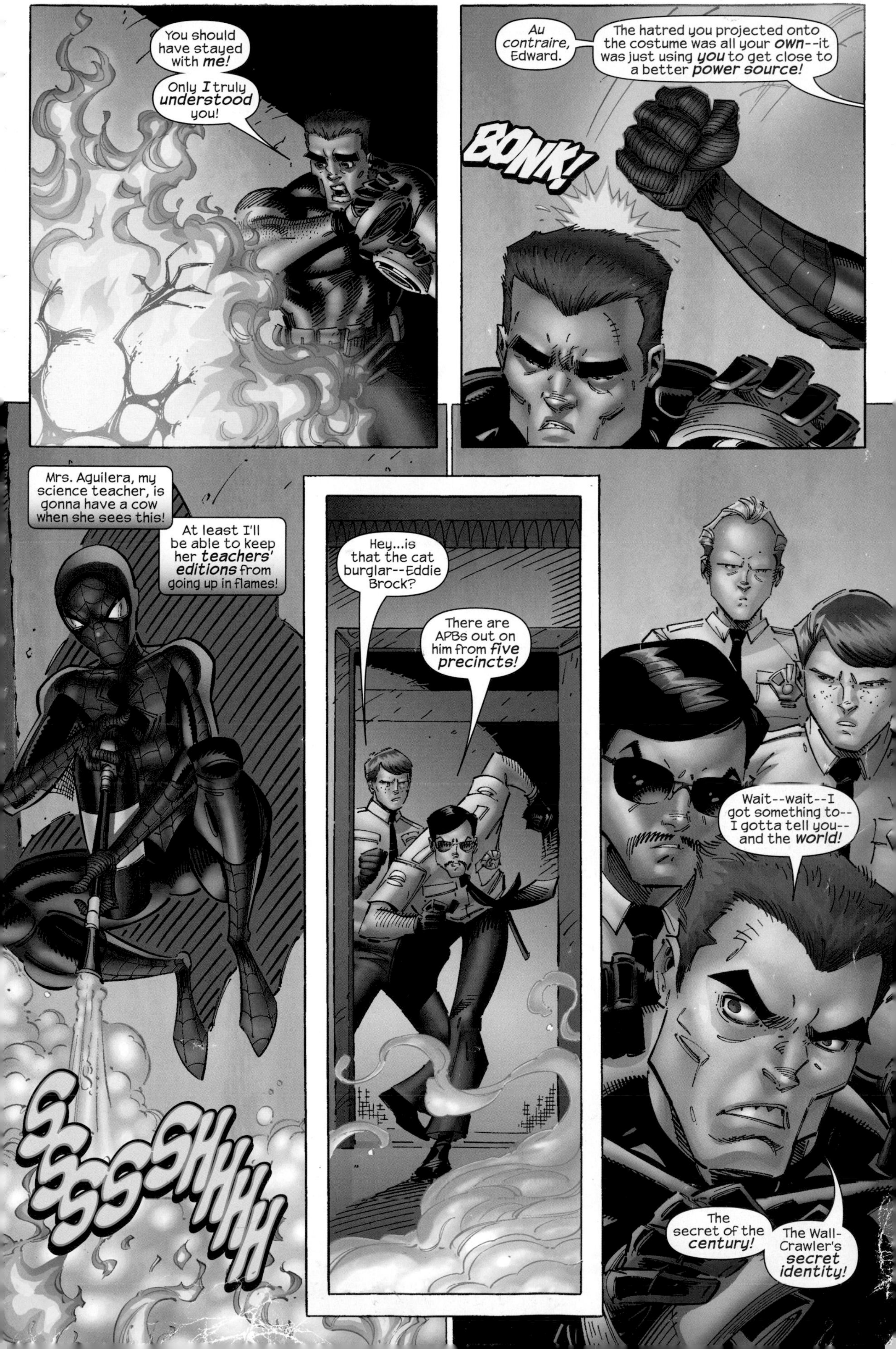
You should have stayed with me!
Only I truly understood you!
Au contraire, Edward.
The hatred you projected onto the costume was all your own--it was just using you to get close to a better power source!
BONK!
Mrs. Aguilera, my science teacher, is gonna have a cow when she sees this!
At least I'll be able to keep her teachers' editions from going up in flames!
SSSSSHHHHH
Hey...is that the cat burglar--Eddie Brock?
There are APBs out on him from five precincts!
Wait--wait--I got something to--I gotta tell you--and the world!
The secret of the century!
The Wall-Crawler's secret identity!

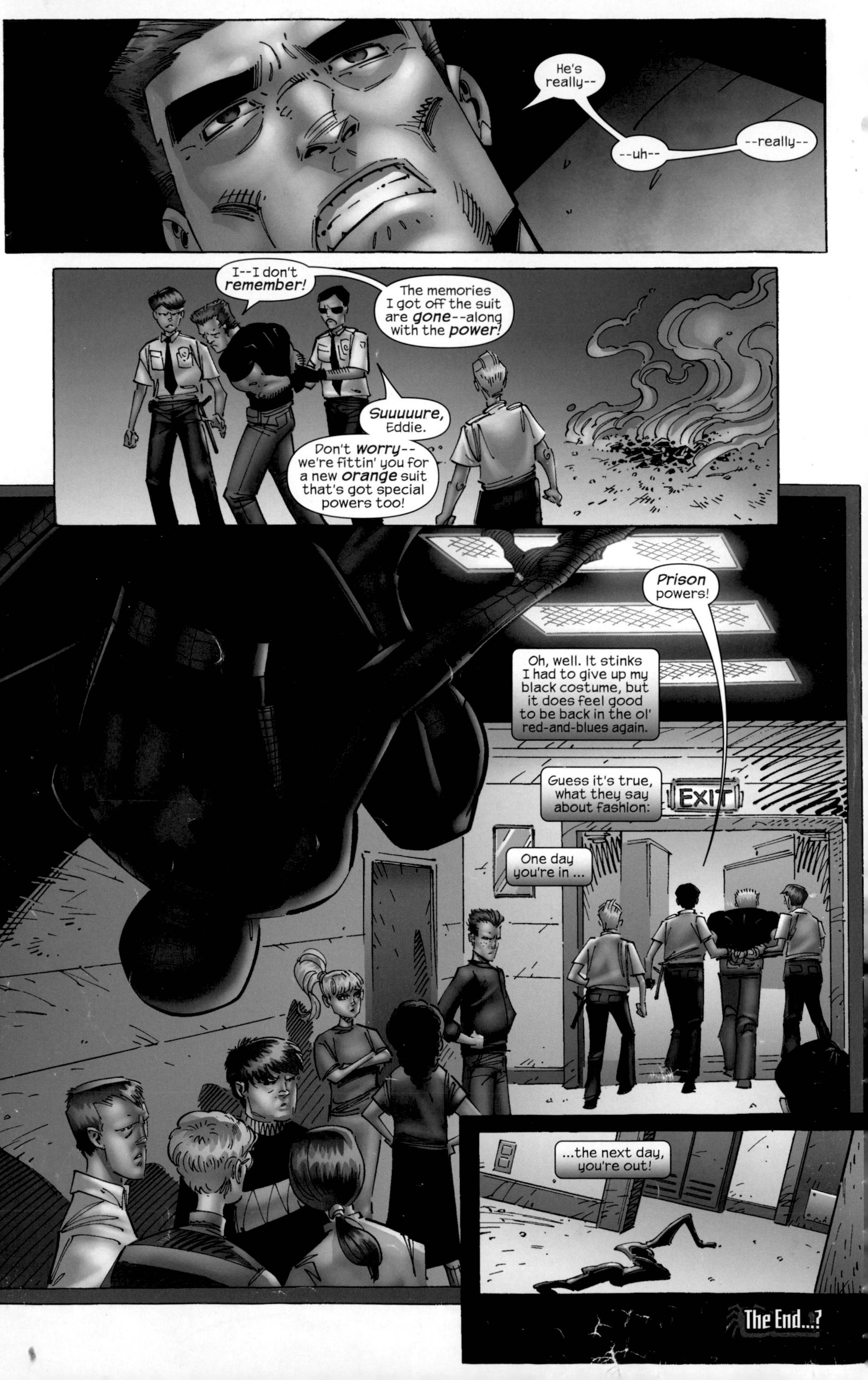
He's really--
--uh--
--really--
I--I don't remember!
The memories I got off the suit are gone--along with the power!
Suuuuure, Eddie.
Don't worry--we're fittin' you for a new orange suit that's got special powers too!
Prison powers!
Oh, well. It stinks I had to give up my black costume, but it does feel good to be back in the ol' red-and-blues again.
Guess it's true, what they say about fashion:
EXIT
One day you're in ...
...the next day, you're out!
The End...?